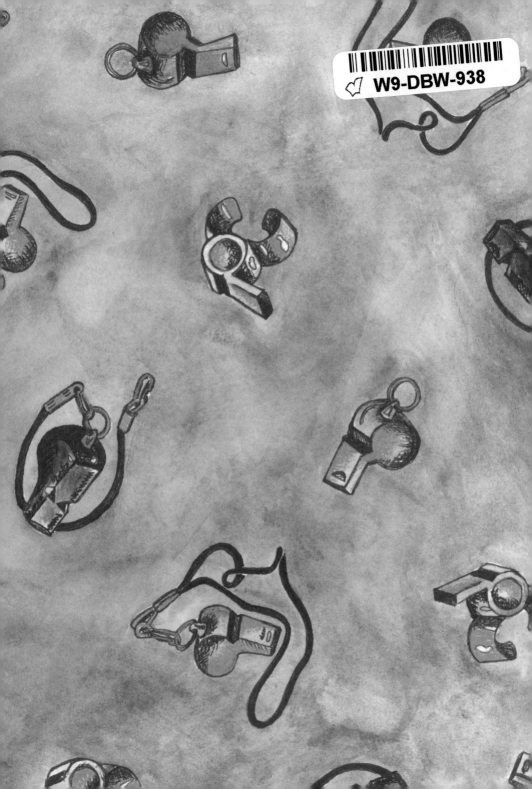
W9-DBW-938

Drop the Puck
Shoot for the Cup

THE OFFICIAL ADVENTURES

Written by Jayne J. Jones Beehler

Illustrated by Katrina G. Dohm

To: Ethan
Smile!!

DROP THE PUCK—SHOOT FOR THE CUP: THE OFFICIAL ADVENTURES © copyright 2016 by Jayne J. Jones Beehler and Katrina G. Dohm. All rights reserved. No part of this book may be reproduced in any form whatsoever, by photography or xerography or by any other means, by broadcast or transmission, by translation into any kind of language, nor by recording electronically or otherwise, without permission in writing from the author, except by a reviewer, who may quote brief passages in critical articles or reviews.

ISBN 13: 978-1-63489-012-0
LCCN: 2015950960
Printed in the United States of America
First Printing: 2015

20 19 18 17 16   5 4 3 2 1

Book design and typesetting by Tiffany Daniels.

Wise Ink Creative Publishing
837 Glenwood Avenue
Minneapolis, MN 55405
wiseinkpub.com

To order, visit www.itascabooks.com or call 1-800-901-3480.
Reseller discounts available.

"*The Official Adventures Series books are terrific heart-warming stories that celebrate hockey, family and children with special needs! Our family loves these hockey tales that teach life lessons and encourages everyone to treat others with respect.*"

— Bridget and Matt Cullen, Pittsburgh Penguins Center

"*This is a very worthwhile read that contains life lessons beyond the rink. It's a great pickup and I especially appreciate that it includes Blaine, a special needs character.*"

— Mike Hickey, President, American Special Hockey Association

"*Drop the Puck, Shoot for the Cup is a great read for hockey players, like me. It gives such a good perspective on what it's like to be a young hockey player from Minnesota. And, I love all the characters, especially Lukey!*"

— Luke Delzer, Pee Wee Hockey Player, Rogers Youth Hockey Association

"*I'm honored to play a small role supporting the life lessons taught in Drop the Puck, Shoot for the Cup. The real story is about Blaine, who is truly a special person to be cherished in the game of life. I hope everyone who reads the book loves it as much as I did. And remember, girls rule and boys drool!*"

— Avery Hakstol, Youth Hockey Player

To endless hockey games on the tele, shared with our past and present hockey players.

A Note from Jayne and Katrina

The adventures of Blaine and Cullen continue with this heartwarming tale that will make you laugh out loud, smile, and cheer for Hockeytown USA! Blaine was born with Down syndrome and has special needs. Down syndrome is a genetic disorder that can cause physical growth delays, characteristic facial features, and mild to moderate intellectual disability. Blaine's speech at times can be stuttering, slurring, and repetitive.

And the story goes...
for the love of the game.

CHAPTER 1

First Goal

The snow was quickly piling up outside their living room window. Inside, Luke and his dad watched the Minnesota State High School League Boys' Hockey Tournament.

"Dad, do you remember playing in the state tourney?" Luke asked as he grabbed a handful of popcorn.

"Do you remember scoring your first goal?" his dad half-jokingly answered.

"Of course I do. It's every hockey player's dream to play in the best high school tourney in the country! We may have lost, but it was an honor to play in the big show!"

Suddenly, with no warning, their hockey tub of popcorn fell to the ground as Stanley made a quick maneuver.

"Ugh! When will Stanley Cup learn he's not little anymore?" grumbled Luke.

"He can't shake. He can't roll over. But that bulldog can watch television on command," Luke's dad added as they cleaned up the popcorn mess.

"And Dad, I do remember my first goal!" snickered Luke.

"You should remember it! First night of hockey practice, and you get a goal and five stitches across your chin!" reminisced Luke's dad.

"Besides the stitches, did I lose my front

Lukey ~ first hockey night!

tooth, like the pros?" asked Luke as he tossed popcorn above his head and tried to catch it in his mouth.

"No, Alex Ovechkin, you didn't. But as the doctor stitched up your chin, you looked at me and asked if you could go back the next night for practice," his dad remembered with a smile.

"And . . . you said, 'Absolutely, Wayne Gretzky. Absolutely,'" Luke stated while raising a thumbs up.

"Not exactly as I remember it," his dad said with a laugh. "But I did understand your love for hockey. It's been in your blood since the first time I tied up your skates and put you on the ice. Never lose your love for the game, Lukey."

"Not a chance, Dad," Luke affirmed as he pet Stanley. "Didn't I get a hat trick in my first game?" he asked.

"Yes, you did. And I don't think you've scored one since!" His dad chuckled.

Luke got up from the couch to stretch. Stanley mimicked Luke's every move.

"I hope we have a snow day tomorrow! It'd be sweet to stay home and watch high school hockey all day with Stanley."

Luke peeked out the window to watch the snow fall, but something else caught his eye.

"Unbelievable. They are unbelievable." Luke raised his arms in exasperation as he quickly found his coat, snow pants, and snow boots.

"You going somewhere?" his dad questioned.

Stanley began to bark.

"Shush," Luke ordered. "It's just Cullen and Blaine."

"Are they coming over to watch hockey?" his dad asked.

"No," Luke said with a giggle. "Come see! It's a blizzard out there, but Cullen is shooting slap shots on Blaine against their garage door! Look at Blaine's homemade goalie pads!"

"Only in Minnesota," Luke's dad groaned.

Luke reached down for his boots as Stanley patiently waited by the door.

"You can come out too, Stanley, but no chasing or biting the puck!" Luke pointed at him. "Dad, tell me later how this barn burner ends. I'll be back for game two. I need to teach our neighbors a few of my hockey tricks," Luke stated as he started out the door. Stanley followed.

"Take it easy on . . . um . . ." His dad hesitated.

"On Stanley?" Luke joked.

"You know who," his dad replied, closing the door.

CHAPTER 2
Snow Day

Stanley dashed and jumped over snowbanks to the neighbors' yard. With one final leap, he landed on the icy driveway. His legs sprawled out as he slid past the neighbor boys. The brothers hardly noticed Stanley and didn't stop shooting pucks at their goalie net.

"Stanley, take goal," Luke directed as he gave a high-five to Cullen, the oldest brother. "Two-on-two? Stanley and me. You and you?" Luke pointed and suggested.

The boys hooted. Stanley barked.

"D-d-did you see Ref Rylee and Ref Rosee on T-T-TV?" asked Blaine.

"I did! Our favorite referees calling all those penalties!" Cullen remarked.

Luke grabbed Blaine's hockey stick and slid on the icy driveway.

"They are the b-b-best," Blaine stated as he ducked to avoid Cullen's large snowball.

"Unless Ref Rylee calls you for every stinking penalty, like he does me," exclaimed Cullen.

"You deserve every whistle and call," Luke added.

"Yeah. He kn-kn-knows your number. Even St-St-Stanley knows your nummmber," Blaine said with a giggle.

10

"I bet they'll be reffing our tournament next weekend. This weekend, the state high school tourney. Next weekend, the stars of the state pee wee tourney," Luke remarked as he shot a puck at the garage.

"Whoa. Whoa. Easy on the garage door, Lukey!" Cullen and Blaine's grandmother announced as she came around the corner. "I think you boys will be happy to hear the news: 'Hockeytown USA Public Schools closed tomorrow!' Your mom and dad picked a great week for their winter vacation!"

All three boys stopped suddenly in their snow-packed tracks. They cheered in unison.

"Is the first game over yet?" Cullen asked his grandma.

"Just finished. They just interviewed Ref Rylee on TV. He and Ref Rosee are working to require all youth players to wear STOP patches on their jerseys."

"Wh-wh-why?" Blaine questioned, now shivering from the stop in hockey action.

"Isn't that to remind players about the dangers of checking from behind?" Luke inquired.

"Yes! Exactly, Lukey! In the heat of the game, sometimes players forget it's just a game. They crash each other into the boards when checking, resulting in serious injury," Grandma replied.

"Speaking of the heat of the game,

could Blaine and I watch the next game at Luke's place?" Cullen asked.

"You can come too, Grandma," Luke offered with a big smile.

"Thanks, Lukey, but I'll stay here to make sure Grandpa has company. You boys come right home after the game is over. No horseplay or monkeying around. We need zero injuries before next weekend's tourney," Grandma reminded.

"Nooo school!" Blaine cheered again. He reached out to hug his grandma.

The boys ran to Luke's house. Stanley tagged along, wagging his stubby tail.

CHAPTER 3

Tourney Traditions

"Hey, Coach—did you hear the news?" Cullen asked.

"Big news? You're going to stay out of the penalty box next weekend?" Luke's dad answered.

"He caaan't, C-C-Coach! Don't p-p-press our luck," snorted Blaine.

"No, Dad. There's no school tomorrow! Snow day!" Luke cheered.

"We can watch tonight's 'nightcap' game, sleep in, then play hockey all day tomorrow!" Cullen reasoned.

"Right after you shovel off the driveway!" Luke's dad added.

The boys groaned.

"You fellas missed a barn burner in the last matchup," Luke's dad bragged.

"C-C-Coach, did you see Ref Rylee and Ref Rosee on TV?" asked Blaine.

"I did. They're my favorites." Luke's dad winked.

"Of course, my brother would be BFFs with the referees!" Cullen said with a laugh.

The three boys sprawled out on blankets across Luke's living room floor.

On the television screen, they could see Ref Rylee skate onto the ice for the evening's last quarterfinal game. The ice cracked as he glided on each edge. The team captains gathered near center ice. Ref Rylee shook their hands and explained his expectation for good sportsmanship, fair play, and friendly competition. Within minutes, the teams lined up on their blue lines. Each team's roster was officially announced.

"Love the flow," Cullen said with a giggle as he pointed to a player's old-school mullet.

"The state tourney is the crown jewel of hockey hair," Luke's dad agreed.

Ref Rylee gave Ref Rosee his usual thumbs up, which was his sign for her to start the game.

"Drrrop the puck, Ref Rosee!" shouted Blaine.

The game remained scoreless after three regulation periods. The shots were tied at just twenty per team.

"Bonus hockey for the normal price of admission," Ref Rylee commented to the game-clock operator as he took a minute to catch his breath.

The game was spirited, and the arena was loud with the student sections and bands trying to outcheer each other.

"This is how champions are made," Luke's dad stated. "You should call your grandma," he added to Blaine and Cullen. "This game could go into at least triple overtime. Official hockey tourney sleepover!"

"Dad, your state hockey championship game went double overtime, right?" questioned Luke.

"Yes, it did," he said quickly.

"B-b-but you didn't w-w-win," chimed in Blaine.

"We lost on a power play goal after my tripping penalty. It stung. We were so close to being crowned state champs," he replied.

"Did your teammates b-b-blame you?" Blaine questioned.

"You win as a team. You lose as a team," Luke's dad answered diplomatically.

"Did you stay on the ice to shake

hands? Or did you head right to the locker room?" Cullen inquired.

"Was it hard, Dad, to watch them raise their championship trophy? Did they get medals? They took home all the hardware," Luke quickly blurted before his dad could answer.

"It burned. But we shook hands like all good athletes do," he said.

No penalties were called in the overtime periods. The shots on goal remained low. Luke's dad looked around the living room floor. The boys were all sound asleep. It was nearing three o'clock in the morning. Unlike the boys, who had an unscheduled day off, he had to get up for work. But he couldn't turn off the game. He watched every play. It was as if he were skating with his state tournament team again.

Ref Rosee skated to center ice. She dropped the puck, opening the fourth overtime period.

Luke woke up. He looked at the television. He nudged the brothers, waking them up too.

Just as Blaine opened his eyes, it happened. A breakaway followed by a three-on-one. A pounding fast slap shot. Five hole. Goal!

Everyone cheered. Stanley barked.

The traditional handshake followed as Ref Rylee and Ref Rosee watched with pride.

"Next weekend," Luke's dad said, "we shake hands, boys. No matter what, we shake hands and hold our heads high," he reminded with pride.

The boys listened. Stanley snored loudly. The boys and Luke's dad laughed as he tossed a pillow at him.

CHAPTER

4

Jeers vs. Cheers

Ref Rylee and Ref Rosee skated off the ice. They walked straight ahead to the officials' locker room. They knew they called a fair game. But they also knew that in close games, it wasn't unusual for the referees to hear yells and boos voicing opinions of missed or bad calls.

"Emotions can run higher in the wee

hours of the morning," Ref Rylee stated while pulling off his skates.

"Not only emotions, but also hockey parents in general." Ref Rosee gave a half laugh.

"When you have both teams' coaches, players, and fans upset with calls, then you know you're doing your job," he responded while stuffing his equipment bag.

"Then I must be doing my job well!" Ref Rosee said with a full laugh.

They walked out of the locker room together. They headed into the arena's concourse, looking for an exit.

"Hey—look! It's two blind mice!" yelled a fan.

"You can borrow my glasses, stripes! You missed a great game!" yelled another fan.

"Ref Rylee! Ref Rosee! Sir? Ma'am? Excuse me?" an unfamiliar voice yelled

from the other side of the concourse.

Ref Rylee and Ref Rosee both stopped. They looked in opposite directions. They were startled to see a young man in a wheelchair wheeling as fast as he could toward them.

"Hi, I'm Rylee," Ref Rylee said while reaching out to shake the young man's hand.

"And I'm Rosee," she added with a bright smile.

"It's awesome to meet you both. I feel so honored. I'm Matthew Acerllo. Everyone calls me 'Ace'. Thank you, from the bottom of my heart, for your work and leadership in reducing checking from behind injuries. It really means the world to me," Ace said while shaking Ref Rylee's hand tightly.

"Ace? I was wondering if that was you from the distance. Last night on the evening news, they replayed the clip of your injury. How are you feeling?" Ref Rylee asked.

"It's been exactly two years. As you might recall, I was playing here in the state championship game. In the intensity, I got checked from behind. The hit wasn't on purpose. I spent weeks in the hospital unable to move. Here's the great news:

I'm about to finish my first year of college. I want to be a team doctor. And I hope to coach," Ace answered proudly.

"That's just great!" Ref Rosee encouraged.

"You are my heroes! Keep up the great work," Ace thanked again.

"I'm proud of you, Ace," Ref Rylee called after him.

"For the many boos and jeers we hear, it's thrilling to meet players like Ace," closed Ref Rylee.

"Yes, it makes it all worth it," Ref Rosee shared.

CHAPTER

5

Mount State of Hockey

"**Y**ou can't even see our goalie net!" Cullen told Blaine as the boys stared out the window, amazed by the snowfall.

"I think we got a foot," Luke estimated.

"Try nineteen inches," Luke's dad corrected.

"W-w-wow!" Blaine hooted.

"We're snowed in. All day. All night.

Hockey tourney on the tele," Cullen cheered.

"Add in pizza for breakfast, lunch, and supper!" Luke said with a laugh.

"Annnd b-b-building a snow f-f-fort," Blaine added.

"That's the recipe for a perfect day!" Luke declared.

Ref Rylee woke up to his hotel room telephone ringing.

"Hello," he answered half asleep.

"Well, I sure didn't expect that text message this morning," Ref Rosee stated quickly.

"Text? What text?" Ref Rylee asked, confused.

"Roads are closed. There's no travel across the state. So as is tradition, the tourney goes on! We're reffing the semifinals tonight and the championship tomorrow night!" Rosee said with excitement.

"We are?" he questioned.

"We just made it to the big show! Meet me in the hotel lobby!" Ref Rosee continued before hanging up.

Ref Rylee lay stunned on his bed. Hockey referees wait years to be called upon for the state tourney. And normally they don't ref back-to-back tournament games. He was quickly reminded of his father's words: "Hard work, commitment, and a positive attitude always pay off."

"I can barely walk. This snow is so deep," Luke complained as Cullen and Blaine followed with shovels.

"It's p-p-past my knees, up-p-p to my ch-ch-chin," Blaine said with a giggle.

"Look at that snow pile the plow made." Cullen pointed kitty-corner across the street.

The three boys ran over and measured themselves next to the gigantic pile.

"Wow! That's awesome and huge!" Luke exclaimed.

"I just saw a television special on snow sculpturing. It reminds me of Mount Rushmore," Luke offered.

"M-M-Mount Rushmore is in S-S-South D-D-Dakota," Blaine corrected.

"I know, silly. But look—don't you see it? I see four faces in this special snow pile," Luke detailed.

"Since when do you watch shows about snow sculpting? I thought your TV only got hockey games," Cullen joked.

"Gentlemen, I think we should make Mount State of Hockey! We need buckets of hot water, food coloring, shovels, and muscle," Luke ordered.

"I'mmm in!" Blaine yelled with energy, flexing his biceps. "I, I, I think," he added.

"Whatever you wish, captain," Cullen told Luke with a smirk.

"Give me a minute. My creative juices

are flowing," Luke stated with his eyes moving back and forth over the snow pile.

The two brothers rolled their eyes at each other. But they were excited to join Luke in sculpting.

The three boys worked into the afternoon, breaking only for design decisions, lunch, and sporadic snack and water breaks. Grandma and Luke's dad enjoyed watching the boys playing outside in an imaginative, old-fashioned way.

"We should get a big blanket for our sculpture unveiling," Luke pondered as he did some last-minute finishing touches.

"I'm just finishing up Zach Parise's eyes," worked Cullen.

Luke's dad came over with his video camera. As usual, Stanley followed closely as to not miss anything. Blaine waved to the camera proudly as Cullen petted Stanley.

"Luke, can you tell me who and what we have here?" asked his dad in a news reporter's tone while holding out a hockey stick like a microphone.

The boys laughed. Stanley barked.

"We are live on location tonight from the State of Hockey—America's hockey capitol—for the unveiling of Mount State of Hockey!" Luke announced in an overdramatic voice. "We've got the faces of Herb Brooks! T. J. Oshie! Zach Parise! and Matthew 'Ace' Acerllo!"

Grandma joined in with the boys' clapping and cheering. Blaine was moved to a case of the giggles. Stanley barked again.

"That's quite the lineup!" Luke's dad continued as he played make-believe reporter.

"Yes," Cullen stated loudly as he pushed Luke aside, stealing the hockey stick microphone and spotlight. "It was an induction of hockey's best tonight. They should be proud! Making it to Mount State of Hockey is like winning the Cup," he announced.

Luke's dad recorded the entire on-location skit.

Just before dusk, the boys came inside along with their cold mittens, snow-packed boots, and frozen snow pants. They warmed up quickly with hot chocolate and cookies.

Soon the boys all cheered out loud when they saw Ref Rylee and Ref Rosee introduced during the pregame festivities. They didn't leave the couch as they watched every play, every period, and every feature story that was broadcast during both games.

While they watched, Luke's dad grabbed his laptop and secretly submitted their Mount State of Hockey video online to the tourney broadcasters. Although many traditions remained from his own state tourney days, things were now very high-tech. The broadcasters were requesting pictures and videos for a "State of Hockey Fan Memories" contest. He had his fingers and hockey sticks crossed in hopes the boys would win!

CHAPTER 6
Championship Trophy

"**W**e should invite our entire team over to watch tonight's championship game," Luke's dad suggested to the boys.

"We c-c-could order p-p-pizza," Blaine suggested quickly.

"Our usual?" Luke's dad asked while pouring himself some orange juice.

"Yes, four large Canadian Maple

Leafs. I can already taste the Canadian bacon with half mushrooms and half green olives." Luke mimicked tasting an imaginary slice.

"Wait—our entire team? That means Avery and Paisley need to be invited," Cullen whined.

Stanley barked.

"That's right. Avery and Paisley are part of our team," Luke's dad enforced, giving Cullen a careful look.

"I, I, I like themmm," Blaine proudly announced.

"I like how fast Avery skates. She can skate circles around you-know-who!" Luke jolted and high-fived Blaine while pointing at Cullen.

"Around you?" Cullen quickly shot back.

"Don't forget: Avery is our third-best scorer and Paisley is our fourth! And her dad plays in the National Hockey League!" Luke's dad interjected.

"They're our first- and second-best scorers with ponytails," Cullen laughed as he grabbed Stanley.

"You'd look good with a ponytail," Luke stated while fixing Cullen's hair.

"I th-th-think p-p-pigtails," Blaine joked.

Luke's dad shook his head, looking again at Cullen in particular. "Avery and Paisley are your teammates, boys. Don't ever speak poorly of your teammates. Now, Luke, you text the girls. I'll order four large Canadian Maple Leafs to be delivered before puck drop," his dad suggested.

"This arena is already going off. I can barely hear my own whistle," Ref Rosee expressed as she shouted over the noise from the pregame festivities.

"Don't you worry—I can blast this whistle louder than any cheering section!" Ref Rylee said and then demonstrated.

The pair skated to center ice.

"You ready to drop the puck on this championship game?" Ref Rylee asked.

"I was born ready," she tossed back while pointing to both teams' goalies.

"P-P-Paisley, look who's r-r-refereeing!" Blaine stated, pointing to the television.

"Ref Rosee and Ref Rylee! That's terrific!" Paisley roared.

"I love it! Ref Rosee is at the big show!" Avery clapped, startling Stanley.

"Maybe someday you girls could referee a game together," Cullen said with a snicker.

"Referee? I'll be playing for the University of North Dakota. And Paisley will be skating for the University of Minnesota. If you play your cards right, maybe we can get you half-priced tickets for a game," Avery proposed without taking a breath.

Stanley barked.

"Now that's what I call a full house," Luke said, nodding at the packed arena on television.

"Standing room only!" Paisley agreed.

"I bet even Ref Rylee is nervous," Cullen pondered.

"Dad, were you nervous playing in the big game?" Luke asked.

"A good dose of nerves is healthy. It makes you play your best," Luke's dad answered.

"Before every game, my dad tells me, 'Just do your best and play with joy, knowing that the game is in your blood and the blood is in your game,'" Paisley offered.

"Trustworthy advice from an NHLer," Luke's dad stated as he rose to his feet and stretched at the end of the first period.

"Close match," Ref Rosee quickly told Ref Rylee.

"Just how a championship game should be played!" Ref Rylee responded while squinting at the TV monitor in the officials' locker room.

"What are you looking at so closely?" Ref Rosee asked.

"Look at that video. Isn't that Blaine, Cullen, and Luke from the Hockeytown USA Pee Wees?" Ref Rylee asked.

"Dad! Dad! DAD!" yelled Luke as he shot up fast and stared at the TV.

"That's usss! H-h-holy m-m-moly!" Blaine shouted.

"Oh my jeepers! Oh my jeepers!" Avery howled pointing at the screen.

"Quiet! No one say a word," Cullen ordered while standing and moving toward the TV.

Luke turned up the volume.

"We had many excellent entries for our State of Hockey video and photo contest," announced the sports reporter. "Your pictures and videos showcased your love of the game. But one video, shall I say, really took the State of Hockey to a new level."

Their video began to play. The boys and girls all stood motionless.

"I, I, I never w-w-won anything b-b-before. I want a m-m-medal!" Blaine shouted while swaying from left to right.

"Sh!" Cullen hushed.

"Congratulations to Blaine, Cullen, and Luke of the Hockeytown USA Pee Wees!" the reporter proclaimed. "We couldn't have made a better Mount State of Hockey ourselves. As our contest winners, you and your youth hockey team will be watching next year's championship game from your own in-arena suite."

"We won!" Cullen shouted.

"Dad, did you send in our video?" Luke asked.

"I certainly did! I was proud of your creativity, spirit, and hard work," he answered.

"I c-c-can't believe it. Weee were on TV! You th-th-think Ref Rylee saw us?" Blaine raised the question with a wide grin.

"Holy ice cream buckets! We get to watch from a suite next year!" Avery fist-bumped Paisley.

"First you'll have to make the team next year," Cullen corrected.

"That'll be easy!" Avery responded.

"We're famous!" Paisley exclaimed. "My phone is blowing up with texts and social media!" Luke giggled, looking at his cell phone buzzing with notifications.

"All right, all-stars—back to the championship game! Who will bring home the trophy?" Luke's dad asked.

"The next team who scores will win," Avery said with confidence.

Cullen shrugged his shoulders while petting Stanley.

The game now over, the two referees watched as the second-place team received their silver medals.

Ref Rylee skated over to Ref Rosee. "It's always fun to officiate a hard-played game, but it's tough to see a team lose the championship by one goal," he said.

"It's all a part of the game and our love

for the game. You win some and, of course, you lose some," Ref Rosee assured him.

"They might not realize it, but second place at state is far from losing," Ref Rylee affirmed.

"And sometimes it's the losses that teach you more lessons," Ref Rosee agreed.

The lights darkened in the arena. A spotlight shone on the ice, and a long red carpet covered center ice to the boards. Ref Rosee and Ref Rylee followed the spotlight's glow. They were surprised to see Matthew Acerllo carrying the championship trophy on his lap as he wheeled himself out to center ice. Wearing white gloves on both his hands, Ace raised the trophy above his head. The silent arena blasted into noise and cheering.

In Luke's living room, the teammates

watched as the state champs took the trophy from Ace and raised it for the crowd, the TV cameras, and themselves.

"I can't wait for next weekend, when we play for state," Avery whispered.

"We are a team," Luke agreed.

The teammates formed a huddle.

"We play our hearts out," Cullen offered.

"Everyone in?" Paisley suggested, putting her hand out. The others stacked their hands on top of hers.

"Blaine, you got this?" Avery asked.

Blaine instantly grinned. "On th-th-three: shoot for the C-C-Cup!" Blaine yelled.

"One, two, three—shoot for the Cup!" the teammates shouted while throwing their arms in the air.

CHAPTER 7

Pee Wee Cup Battle

*I*n preparation for their state pee wee hockey tournament, Luke and his team practiced every night. Avery's dad volunteered to help get the team tourney-ready. They even had a few early-morning practices and did two-a-days like the pros.

One day before the tourney, the team gathered once again for practice.

"Team, this is our last practice before

we leave for the state tourney!" Luke's dad announced. "We must play as a team. Every jersey number on this team matters. From Blaine to Paisley, everyone has a role to play, a job to do. Success is determined by the way a team plays as a whole."

Then Luke's dad put down his clipboard and whistle.

"And now we're done practicing," he stated.

"But Dad, we just got to practice. Tomorrow is game day," Luke questioned.

Luke's dad moved the goalie nets to center ice facing each other. "Team, instead of practicing, we're going to do the Minnesota Snowman! I need everyone to line up behind Paisley on the blue line. Cullen, Avery's dad is going to put this stick through the TUUK holders in your skates, and then we're going to hang you between the two nets. Team, your job is to skate hard, do a hockey stop, and spray Cullen with snow!"

"I'mmm not sure about th-th-this, C-C-Coach," Blaine shared.

"I am!" Paisley said with a laugh.

"Me too! A dream come true," Avery joked while taking her place in line.

"Careful, I am the MVP of the team," Cullen rattled off with a grin as the two dads lifted him by the stick through his skates and masterfully positioned the stick across the nets.

"We don't have an MVP, Cullen. We have an MVT, and don't forget it," Luke's dad reminded him.

"MVT?" Cullen questioned.

"Most Valuable Team," Avery's dad answered.

The drill began with roars of giggles and laughter. At the end, Cullen was covered head to toe in snow and rolling on the ice with a good case of the giggles himself.

"Mission accomplished," Luke's dad smiled while ending the fun-filled practice.

The next day, the team arrived at the ice arena where the tourney would be held.

"Cullen and Blaine, look down at the ice!" Luke said as they gathered at the top of the spectator section.

"I see a T-T-TV cameraman! Is our tourrrney on F-F-FSN?" Blaine asked, referring to the local sports network.

"Not yet," Ref Rylee interrupted.

"Ref R-R-Rylee!" Blaine yelled while reaching for a quick hug.

"Hey, Ref Rylee, why is the camera guy on the ice?" Luke questioned.

"Just taping player introductions for the Jumbotron! Speaking of the Jumbotron . . . Cullen, you better watch your penalties. They've got instant replay here!" Ref Rylee winked and walked away.

"W-w-will you say 'Hi, G-G-Grandma' or 'Hi, M-M-Mom,' like the s-s-state hockey players d-d-do?" Blaine asked Cullen.

"He's too cool for that!" Luke bounced back.

"Too cool for school?" asked Paisley, who walked up to the boys with Avery.

"L-l-look, P-P-Paisley," Blaine said while pointing to the on-ice camera crew.

"Shut the rink door! We're on NBC Sports! Grab my phone—quick! No one will believe this!" Avery stated in a sudden panic.

"Simmer down, Erin Andrews! It's just an in-arena camera," Cullen said as he shook his head. "I guess you can't take the Hockeytown USA girl to the big city," he mumbled.

"I can't believe we get to play here!" Paisley said as she looked around the arena in awe.

"It is rad," Luke exclaimed while practicing his stick handling.

"I'm g-g-going to say 'Hi, M-M-Mom'

for the c-c-camera," Blaine still reasoned.

"No one cares about the hockey manager," Cullen whined.

"We do!" Paisley shot back, grabbing Blaine's arm with Avery.

"We, the three of us, have a game to play and win! Let's go!" Avery said as they hustled away.

The young team skated onto the ice, and Blaine took his managerial spot on the team's bench. It was almost game time.

"I, I, I have p-p-pregame j-j-jitters," Blaine told Ref Rosee and Ref Rylee.

"We all get them," Ref Rosee said with a smile. She picked up a bottle from the bench and squirted some water into her mouth.

"Easy! I j-j-just filled th-th-that," Blaine

joked, reaching for the bottle.

"You are America's best hockey manager!" Ref Rylee stated while fist-bumping Ref Rosee.

"I t-t-try to do my best, r-r-right, Coach?" Blaine explained as Luke's dad approached and shook hands with both referees.

"Be ready, Blaine. The camera crew is coming to you after they introduce the rest of the team," Luke's dad shared.

The players lined up, and the camera crew came down the line as each player's name was announced. The teammates smiled as they saw each other on the Jumbotron.

"Hi, M-M-Mom!" Blaine proudly stated into the camera as he heard his name.

"They j-j-just s-s-said, 'B-B-Blaine Ashton, t-t-team mannnager!'" Blaine screeched proudly to Ref Rylee as the camera passed.

"They should have said, 'America's best manager,'" Ref Rylee affirmed as he positioned himself next to the blue line.

Blaine couldn't stop giggling as he raised his arms, waving them to get his mom's attention.

From the stands, his mom smiled. She knew her son was beaming with pride hearing his name announced as a part of the team. For Blaine, the simple pleasures in life were some of his most treasured moments.

The puck dropped! The game got off to a fast start. Before the players knew it, they were through three regulation periods and into overtime. Avery scored a hat trick, and Cullen also had a goal. The score was tied 4 to 4, and only minutes remained in the third and final overtime. If no one scored, the teams would go to the tournament's rule of a mandatory shootout.

Then suddenly, in an intense moment of competitive play, there was a crushing check and a clash of bodies. All play instantly stopped. The young player who had been checked was lying motionless on the ice.

Cullen skated toward his team's bench. He was the one who had delivered the check from behind.

Ref Rosee signaled for a game misconduct penalty against Cullen.

"I didn't check him from behind! He had

the puck, and he fell. I didn't check him!" Cullen argued.

Ref Rylee skated toward the Hockeytown USA team bench. "Coach, you need one of your other players to sit in the penalty box for the five minutes. This player needs to exit the ice," he said, pointing at Cullen.

Luke's dad nodded. "It was a good call, Ref. We are better than that. Emotions are running high in this championship," Luke's dad acknowledged.

Cullen slammed his stick on the glass. He angrily removed his helmet and skated off the ice. This was Cullen's first game misconduct penalty of the season. And a big one!

As he sat in the empty locker room, he felt miserable. He had let his emotions and temper get the best of him. He had let his team down.

CHAPTER 8
The Shootout

The overtime horn sounded. The game remained tied 4 to 4. A champion still hadn't been crowned!

"Dad, we've never practiced a shootout before!" Luke said with panic in the team's huddle.

"Don't worry. Let's just do our best," Luke's dad replied to calm down his nervous young team.

Ref Rosee and Ref Rylee skated over to the team's bench.

"You will get four shooters, Coach. If needed, we will go to another round of shooters," Ref Rylee clarified.

The shootout began. The players on both teams stood up and hung their sticks over the bench, pounding them against the wall after each goalie save. Both goalies were on fire and playing their best hockey of the season. The crowd cheered louder and louder.

Luke's shot missed the net completely.

"Avery, you're up next," Luke's dad ordered.

Paisley slapped Avery's helmet.

"Brrring us home m-m-medals, Avery. I w-w-want a m-m-medal!" Blaine cheered while clapping loudly.

"And the Cup, Avery!" Luke yelled.

Avery skated to center ice. Ref Rosee blew her whistle. Avery didn't move. She took a big deep breath and glanced up to the stands. She saw her grandpa standing up and clapping.

"Go, Avery! Go, Avery, go!" she heard.

She smiled and started to skate with rapid speed. She cut to her left. Glided fast to her right. As the goalie positioned himself for a save to the right, Avery cut a quick edge left. She took a fast shot.

GOAL!

It was a hat trick plus a shootout goal for Avery—and a state victory for the team!

The entire team cleared the bench and rushed onto the ice. They dove on top of each other, making a huge victory pile.

As soon as Cullen heard the ruckus, he skated back onto the ice. He couldn't wait to celebrate with his team. But first, he skated to Ref Rylee and Ref Rosee, reaching to shake their hands.

"I'm sorry for my behavior," he apologized. "How's the ARH All-Star player I checked doing? I hope he's okay."

Ref Rylee and Ref Rosee thanked Cullen.

"The ARH All-Star player will be all right," Ref Rosee stated. "He was shook up, but he shows no signs of injury. He's very lucky," she added in a serious tone.

"There are many dangers with checking from behind. We want all players to remain safe on the ice," Ref Rylee reminded Cullen.

Cullen nodded and shook their hands.

Now Cullen was ready to join his team. He skated over and hugged Blaine. The brothers then joined Avery and

Paisley near center ice as Luke lifted the state pee wee championship cup above his head.

"I, I, I can't w-w-wait for my m-m-medal!" Blaine's face glowed.

"We all can't wait! We did it!" Avery cheered.

As Cullen patted Avery on top of her helmet, he smiled. "Way to go, Avery. I'm proud to be part of your MVT!"

ASK THE OFFICIALS
Rylee and Rosee's
Referee Resources

Important Words to Learn

barn burner: An extremely exciting hockey game or competition.

checking: Knocking an opponent, sometimes against the boards or to the ice, by using the hip or body.

checking from behind: To check or push an opponent from behind, which can result in injury.

hat trick: When one player scores three goals in a game.

jeers: Insulting words directed at someone.

maneuver: A movement or series of movements requiring skill and care.

regulation: The standard period of time in a hockey game, excluding overtime.

shootout: A means of resolving a tie in hockey, in which selected players from each team alternately take individual shots on a goal defended only by a goalie.

snicker: A laugh someone tries to hide.

sportsmanship: Fair play, respect for opponents, and polite behavior when competing in hockey or other competition.

MEET JAYNE AND KATRINA

Jayne wears many helmets, including college professor, lawyer, author, wife, mother, and advocate for individuals with disabilities.

Katrina displays her high energy and love for life each day as an artist, designer, illustrator, art educator, event planner, wife, and mother.

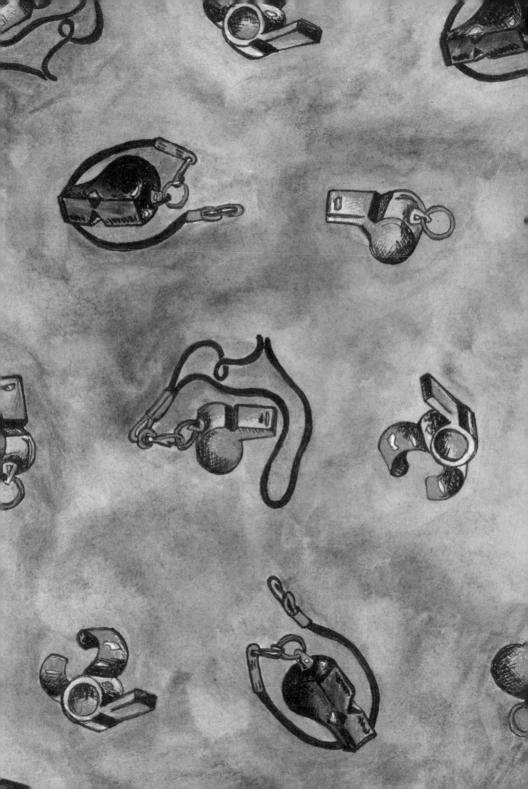